Blue Glasses

First published in 2009
by Wayland

Text copyright © Louise John
Illustration copyright © Miriam Latimer

Wayland
338 Euston Road
London NW1 3BH

Wayland Australia
Level 17/207 Kent Street
Sydney, NSW 2000

Series Editor: Louise John
Cover design: Paul Cherrill
Design: D.R.ink
Consultant: Shirley Bickler

A CIP catalogue record for this book is available from the British Library.

ISBN 9780750259408

Printed in China

Wayland is a division of Hachette Children's Books,
an Hachette UK Company

www.hachette.co.uk

Blue Glasses

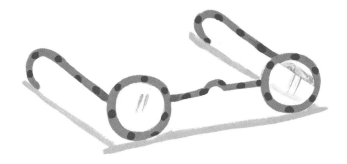

Written by Louise John
Illustrated by Miriam Latimer

WAYLAND

"Look," said Poppy.
"I can see our bus!"

"No," said Mum.
"That is not our bus."

7

"Look," said Poppy.
"I can see our house."

"No, Poppy, that is not
our house," said Mum.

9

"Look," said Dad.
"The football is on TV.
Come and see
the football."

"I can see our team," said Poppy.

"No," said Dad. "That is not our team."

"Come on," said Dad.
"We are going to get
some glasses for you."

"Look," said Dad.

"I can see **c** for cat," said Poppy.

"No," said Dad. "That is **a** for apple."

"Red glasses, green glasses or blue glasses?" said Poppy.

"Blue glasses," said Dad.

19

"Yes, blue glasses," said Poppy. "Blue glasses for me!"

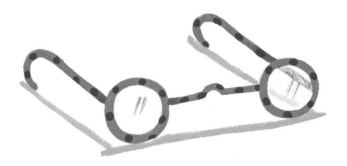

Guiding a First Read
Blue Glasses

It is important to talk through the book with the child before they read it alone. This prepares them for the way the story unfolds, and allows them to enjoy the pictures as you both talk naturally, using the language they will later encounter when reading. Read them the brief overview, and then follow the suggestions below:

The high frequency words in this title are:
can   come   I   is   look   Mum
no   our   said   see

1. Talking through the book
Poppy thinks she can see well, but Mum and Dad realise that she needs to have her eyes tested.

'Blue Glasses' is the title of this book.
On page 4, Poppy is at the bus stop. She tells Mum, "I can see our bus." Do you think it is her bus? Turn over the page. No, it's not.

Continue through the book, guiding the discussion to fit the text, as the child looks at the illustrations.

On page 14, Dad and Poppy are going out.
What do you think they are going to get?

And which glasses does Dad choose on page 18? Turn the page. Were you right?
Does Poppy like the blue glasses too?

2. A first reading of the book

Ask the child to read the book independently and point carefully underneath each word (tracking), while thinking about the story.

Work with the child, prompting them. Praise their careful tracking, attempts to correct themselves and their knowledge of letters, sounds and punctuation, for example:

> **You said, "That is not OUT bus." Does that make sense? What do you think it could be instead? Have another look.**
> **I like the way you sounded out the word apple. You made Poppy sound really excited when you read that. Well done!**

3. Follow-up activities

· Select two high frequency words, and ask the child or group to find them throughout the book. Discuss the shape of the letters and the letter sounds.

· To memorise the words, ask the child to write them in the air, then write them repeatedly on a whiteboard or on paper, leaving a space between each attempt.

4. Encourage

· Reading the book again – with expression.

· Drawing a picture based on the story.

· Writing one or two sentences using the practised words.

START READING is a series of highly enjoyable books for beginner readers. **The books have been carefully graded to match the Book Bands widely used in schools.** This enables readers to be sure they choose books that match their own reading ability.

Look out for the Band colour on the book in our Start Reading logo.

The Bands are:

	Pink Band 1
	Red Band 2
	Yellow Band 3
	Blue Band 4
	Green Band 5
	Orange Band 6
	Turquoise Band 7
	Purple Band 8
	Gold Band 9

START READING books can be read independently or shared with an adult. They promote the enjoyment of reading through satisfying stories supported by fun illustrations.

Louise John is really the editor of Start Reading, but wanted to see how she liked writing books, too. It was quite tricky, but she found that eating lots of chocolate biscuits made her think better! She tries out her ideas on her daughter, Amelia, who tells her if they are any good or not!

Miriam Latimer enjoys illustrating and writing stories for children. She carries her sketchbook and pens with her everywhere she goes, which make her handbag very heavy. She likes to sketch people in cafés and train stations but, if they notice, she pretends to be drawing something else!